THE GAY PRETENDER

Gay Romance Erotica

WARNING

This book contains sexually explicit scenes and adult language. It may be considered offensive to some readers. This book is for sale to adults ONLY.

* * * * * * * * * * * * * * * * * * *

Please store your files wisely where they cannot be accessed by underage readers.

Please feel free to send me an email. Just know that these emails are filtered by my publisher. Good news is always welcome.

Dick Parker - **dick_parker@awesomeauthors.org**

About the Publisher

4Fun Publishing, a member of **BLVNP Incorporated**, 340 S. Lemon #6200, Walnut CA 91789, info@blvnp.com / legal@blvnp.com
NOTE: Due to the highly emotional reaction of some people to works of erotic fiction, any email sent to the above address that contains foul language or religious references is automatically deleted by our anti-spam software and will not be seen. All other communications are welcome.

DISCLAIMER

Please don't be stupid and kill yourself. This book is a work of FICTION. Do not try any new sexual practice that you find in this book. It is fiction and not to be confused with reality. Neither the author nor the publisher or its associates assume any responsibility for any loss, injury, death or legal consequences resulting from acting on the contents in this book. Every character in this book is over 18 years of age. The author's opinions are not to be construed as the opinions of the publisher. The material in this book is for entertainment purposes ONLY. Enjoy.

The Gay Pretender
Gay Romance Erotica

By: Dick Parker

ISBN: 978-1-62761-700-0

Chapter One

I was a little nervous as I parked in the lot at the dorm I had been assigned to for the wrestling camp I was attending. I wrestled all four years of high school and my senior year I made it to the State tournament and won my weight class. I was a state champion and it was quite an accomplishment. Soon afterward I got a letter from the University offering me a wrestling scholarship. I had a free ride for a college education and all I had to do was wrestle, something that I loved.

Part of the bargain required me to attend a two-week wrestling camp at the campus in the middle of the summer before school started. I wasn't too worried about the camp because I knew I could wrestle with most anyone and hold my own. I was a little nervous about not being the star anymore.

In high school I was a big deal. I had the best record on the team, and had a lot of attention from fans and all of the girls in school. I'm not saying I'm drop-dead gorgeous but I'm not bad-looking. I've worked out since seventh grade and have a good body with some pretty nice muscles and everything in the right places. I wrestled in my senior year at 145 so I'm not huge but I'm not the littlest guy on the team either.

I do have one thing that I feel makes me stand out and that's my curly light brown hair. I've been accused of curling it but anyone who knows me knows it's been curly since I was a little kid. I wear it a little longer than most wrestlers because it looks damn good. In the summer it gets blond streaks in it and it turns a lot of heads.

I've always been popular and had all kinds of attention because of my wrestling and my looks. There was never a time when any girl I asked to a dance or some party turned me down. But if the truth was known, it was all a sham.

There's only one thing missing from my life. It is one thing that I can't talk about to my friends, and don't know what to do about. With all the attention from girls, I have to pretend that I enjoy it when in reality I hate it. The truth is… I'm gay.

I've known for a long time. I think back to when my pals and I would go to the river and end up skinny-dipping. I loved seeing them naked and watching their little dicks bounce around. Then when we got a little older our dicks got bigger and it turned me on all the more. I loved the little sparse pubes we grew and loved seeing our cocks get bigger and our balls grow up. It turned me on like crazy. But I never acted on it. Oh I jacked off until my dick got sore, but I never touched another boy for fear of being called a gay boy.

I think back to the dozens of times when my pals and I had sleepovers and ended up in a big bed made of blankets on the basement floor. I lay there with half a dozen of my buddies in our underwear wanting so badly to touch one of them but I was terrified to try it. Even with my wrestling pals, I had to be so careful not to get a boner while working out with them or in the shower. It was hell.

So for all the success I've had with wrestling and school, my life is pretty empty. I longed for someone to cuddle within the tent when camping out. I lusted for one of my friend's cocks to suck. But I was still a virgin and as frustrated as it was possible to be.

Now here I was at my college campus. I was used to being the big fish in the pond, and now I was just one of the many little fish. I didn't know what to expect as I carried my duffle bag into the dorm lobby.

There was a man sitting at a desk inside the entry and he smiled at me.

"You must be one of our wrestlers," he said.

"Yes sir, I'm Micah Grant."

He looked at a list and then pointed to a hallway.

"Room 43, down that hall. I think your roommate is there already. Here's your key and meal pass."

He handed me the key and a plastic credit card looking thing and a booklet with rules and instructions for the dorm.

"Nice to have you on the team," he said.

"Thanks. I hope I'll live up to your expectations," I replied.

I picked up my duffel and walked down the hall, took a left and found my room. I could hear music coming from inside.

I opened the door and there sat a kid who must be my roommate. But he didn't look old enough to be in college so I wasn't sure.

"Are you my roommate?" I asked.

"If you're Micah, I'm him," the kid said getting up and walking toward me.

"I'm Micah," I said.

He smiled widely and held out his hand.

"I'm Jason Richards," he said.

Damn he was adorable.

We shook hands and I looked around. The room wasn't real homey. There were two desks near the window, two beds, one on each side of the room, two dressers and two closets.

"Really nice," I said grinning.

"Just like home at the juvenile prison," Jason said.

He helped me unpack and put my stuff away. I watched him and damn he was a hot little shit. He was five foot five at the most. I guessed he weighed around one thirty and he was really well built. His hair was cut in that just-woke-up style and was a sandy brown. He had incredible blue eyes and a cute face with a great smile. He was wearing gym shorts and a tank top and was barefoot.

"So where are you from, Jason?"

"I'm from a little town you never heard of way up north. I was a state regional champion the last three years but never made the state tournament like you did."

"How do you know what I did?"

"Oh I read up on you when I found out you'd be my roommate. You da man Micah."

"So we're new roommates and new friends," I said.

"Cool, so now I'm your friend?"

"I think so. If you want to be."

"Damn straight," he said. He playfully punched me in the stomach. "I think we're gonna be good friends," he said.

"Don't take offense but how old are you?" I asked.

"I'm eighteen and will turn nineteen in a few weeks. You thought I was like twelve?"

I grinned.

"Well maybe not twelve but I thought you were younger than you are. I just turned eighteen and you look a lot younger than I do."

"You know how it is with us little guys who wrestle. We diet and work out to stay under our wrestling weight and sometimes we are a little behind the norm in the maturing process. Don't get me wrong, I'm all man in the dick department."

I laughed.

"I bet you are."

It had been a long drive to the school and I'd gotten up early and skipped my shower so I felt a little grungy.

"I think I'll take a shower," I said.

"Cool I will too."

That kind of surprised me but it didn't hurt my feelings. I was looking forward to seeing this little hot shit naked.

I took off my shoes and socks and jeans and stripped off my shirt. Then I dropped my boxers. Jason made no pretense of watching and took a good look at my dick.

"Ready?" I said wrapping my towel around my waist.

"Yup," he said. He stripped off his tank top. Damn he had nice little tufts of brown hair under his arms. Then he pulled off his shorts and he was commando under them. His cock was really pretty. His pubes were compact and it looked like he trimmed them. He had big balls for such a small guy and his cock hung down three inches or more over his low hanging ball sack. He was circumcised and his cock hung a little to the right making me think he jacked off left-handed.

He wrapped his towel around his waist and grinned.

"What do you think?" he asked.

"Um, about what?"

"You looked at my dick pretty hard. You think it's okay?"

"Oh sorry, I didn't mean to. Yeah, it's a fine dick," I said smiling.

I grabbed my shower kit and he grabbed his and we walked down the hallway. Two other guys were just coming out of the shower. One was a big kid who must have been a heavyweight or one of the higher weights and the other was a mid-weight guy. They stopped and we introduced ourselves. Then Jason and I went into the shower room and dropped our towels.

We walked into the shower. It was a communal shower with eight spigots on the walls with four on each side. I turned one on and Jason turned one on right next to me. We got the temperature right and then got under the water. It felt good with the warm water running down my body. I looked over at Jason and he looked so cute with water running down his cute little body and off his nice cock.

He looked at me and grinned.

"I like being naked," he said.

"Me too. I used to go skinny dipping a lot back home with my buddies," I said.

"Oh cool. I've done that a few times. Ever do it with a girl?"

Shit!

"No, I never got the chance," I said.

"Me either. I just thought that since you're such a good-looking guy you probably had all the pussy you wanted in high school."

"Oh, not so much," I said trying to drop the subject.

"Really? I'd have thought you'd get all kinds of pussy. How big does that cock of yours get when it's hard?"

Jeez.

"Oh it's about six inches," I said.

"Mine's five inches and five eighths."

I laughed.

"Five and 5/8? You must have measured pretty close."

He grinned.

"My friend Tony measured it for me."

Holy shit. He saw my surprise and shrugged.

"Hey, it's no big deal," he said.

"You just surprised me is all," I said.

"You never messed around with a buddy?"

Oh shit this was getting out of hand.

"Not really. You did?"

"Yeah, I hope that doesn't stop us from being friends," he said.

Oh man. I was picturing him with another guy and I started to get a hard-on. I turned my back and hurried to rinse off.

"Are you pissed?" he asked.

"No it's okay. I just... I got to dry off."

He turned off his shower and got his towel. I wrapped my towel around my waist and it was pretty obvious I had a boner. There was a big bulge about the size of a hard cock sticking out in front of my crotch.

Jason looked at it and grinned.

"Spring a boner? Cool, it looks like you've got a nice one."

My face turned red and I nodded.

"You ready?"

He tugged on his cock a few times and then wrapped his towel around his waist.

"Let's go," he said.

We got back to our room and I pulled on some clean boxers and a pair of shorts. Jason farted around for ten minutes sorting through clothes naked. Finally he pulled on some shorts and sleeveless tee shirt.

"So how about some lunch?" he asked.

Chapter Two

We walked to a building a block away that was the food service building for all of the dorms. Since the wrestling camp was the only thing going on right now there weren't many people there.

The food looked pretty good and we took our trays to the dining room. There were about twenty guys scattered around and Jason led me to a table with two other guys sitting at it.

One was a little guy like Jason and the other was a mid-weight. The little guy had to be part Mexican or from some Spanish country. He was real dark with black hair and eyes and a cute little face. He wore his hair kind of long covering his ears and looked really well built. He grinned when Jason and I sat down.

The other one was a blond kid with a messy haircut like Jason's. There were places in his hair where it was really almost white so he'd had that done or it was just natural from the sun. It looked amazing. He had really deep blue eyes and a really handsome face. Everything about his face was perfect, his nose, lips and those gorgeous eyes. He was wearing a very thin-strapped muscle shirt and he had very muscular shoulders and biceps. While he was really well built, he wasn't like some over-muscled gym rat. He was perfect.

"This little shit is Manuel. This big hunk of manhood is Trevor."

I said hi to both of them.

I shook with Manuel and then with Trevor. His grip was firm but his hands soft.

"We call Manuel, Manny," Trevor said.

"Cool, nice to meet you guys," I said. "What weight do you wrestle?" I asked Trevor.

"I've been at 145 but I'm not sure if I'll stay there. I've bulked up a little this summer so I might have to go up one weight."

"I'm 145 too," I said. "We'll probably be practice partners.

"Cool," he said. And then he winked at Jason.

"Manny and I are partners too," Jason said.

"Yeah, we work out together," Manny said and they both started laughing.

I wasn't sure what the joke was but it seemed that I was the only one who didn't get it.

We ate and talked and after we finished, we walked back to the dorm. Manny and Trevor lived one floor above us. We agreed to meet them at 1 o'clock in the entrance to go to a meeting with the coach at the gym.

"So what was all that laughing about?" I asked.

"Oh nothing. Sorry we weren't joking about you. Manny and I have been friends for a couple of years. We met at a wrestling camp one summer and got along really good. We've spent weekends at each other's places since then. Manny lives in the school district next to mine so we're not far away. Trevor and Manny went to the same high school and have been friends for a long time. We've all been friends for a few years. They were just goofing around."

We sat around and talked until just before one and then walked out and met the guys. We were all wearing shorts and tees or tank tops and sandals or flip-flops. It seemed to be the norm for dress at the camp because when we got to the gym the rest of the wrestlers were similarly attired.

I looked around. Damn it was like a flesh market. The gym was full of well-built guys all skimpily dressed and showing off their muscles and a few had on shorts that left little to the imagination in what lain under them. I think all wrestlers get off on showing their bodies off.

The coach had us sit on the mats and he began talking about the training and the upcoming season. Jason and Manny were sitting together and I noticed Manny had his legs crossed in front of him and the head of his dick was showing in the leg of his shorts. It looked like a little turtles-head poking out.

I was enjoying looking at it when Jason shifted around a little and slid his hand in Manny's shorts leg and stroked his cock. Manny grinned and whispered something to him.

Damn. I began getting a boner.

I looked away and tried to think of anything but Manny's cock. I moved my hand to my crotch and pushed my boner down so it wasn't so obvious. When I looked up Trevor was watching me and grinning.

I shrugged my shoulders and he smiled. I guess it didn't bother him that I had a hard-on.

We learned that the first practice would be the next morning at 7 o'clock. Then we all got up and headed back to the dorm. My boner had gone down half way so my cock just hung loose instead of standing up and being real obvious.

Jason and Manny took off running to the dorm and Trevor walked with me.

"Get a little excited back there?" Trevor asked when we were walking down the sidewalk.

"Yeah, I don't know what set it off. You know how it is; sometimes your cock has a mind of its own."

"Yeah I know about that. Mine is hard as much as it's soft. I think I might go back and jack off when we get back."

Wow that surprised me. I wasn't used to someone coming out and saying something like that.

"What about Manny?"

"Jason didn't tell you?"

"He didn't tell me anything about Manny."

"He and Manny are kind of boyfriends."

"No shit? He said they were friends. I guess I didn't think of them being that kind of friends."

"Does that bother you?"

"No, it just surprised me. I have no problem with it."

"Cool. Why don't you come up to my room for a little while? I bet Manny and Jason are having sex right now."

"Well sure, I'd hate to barge in on them."

Really I'd love to walk in and see those two cuties naked and fucking but I didn't want to say that.

I followed Trevor up the stairs. Damn he had a fine ass. We got to his room and he let us in. It looked just like ours.

"Make yourself homely," Trevor said laughing.

I sat on one of the beds and he kicked off his sandals. I kicked mine off too. He had nice looking feet. I must have stared at them too long.

"You into feet?"

"What? Oh I just noticed… I'm, yeah, I guess feet turn me on for some reason."

"Not a problem. I like them too. You've got nice feet Micah."

"Oh thanks," I said. I could feel my face heating up.

"So do you have a girlfriend at home?" he asked.

"No, not right now."

"Break up?"

"Well not really. I kind of dated casually and didn't get a steady girlfriend."

"Spread yourself around then," he said.

"Yeah, I guess. You have one?"

"Nah. I'm ambivalent about them. They're so hard to get along with. There's so much drama with girls. I'm happy being single."

"That's kind of how I feel. Starting college is hard enough without having to worry about the drama of a girlfriend."

"Jacking off is fun anyway," he said.

"Yeah, you've got that right."

"What do you think Manny and Jason are doing?"

"Damn I don't know. Do they do... it?"

He grinned. "I think they've been doing it for a while. Manny tells me that Jason can fuck like a bunny so I think that means they're doing it."

"Wow!"

I felt my cock stirring.

I looked over and Trevor was massaging his cock through his shorts. He looked right at me and didn't try to hide it.

"What do you think?" he asked.

"About? That?" I asked looking at his obvious boner.

"I'm horny. Want to jack off together?"

Oh man. My insides felt like jelly. I wanted to see him naked but was scared to death he might tell someone.

"I've never jacked off with anyone before," I said.
"Really? It's fun, and pretty erotic."

"As long as we keep it between us," I said.

"I'm not telling the team. Come on, let's have some fun."

I nodded and we both stood up. We took our shirts off and I nearly gasped at Trevor's body. It was amazing. Every muscle was pronounced but not huge and bulky. His nipples were tiny like dimes and light brown. He had a treasure trail that disappeared into his shorts.

He hooked his thumbs into the top of his shorts and pulled them down. They slid to the floor and he stepped out of them. His cock was gorgeous. He had a trimmed bush and must have shaved his balls because they were hairless and hung low below his thick cock that stood up toward his belly button. It was a good thick six inches and had a perfect shaped head.

I dropped my shorts and my cock popped up. Mine sticks straight out in front of my pubes. Mine is six inches exactly and pretty thick. Of the few boners I've seen, mine is the fattest I've seen.

"Nice fat cock," Trevor said.

"Yours is really nice too," I said.

We both sat on one of the beds across from each other. Our feet were nearly touching. We began jacking off watching each other.

Trevor moved one of his feet over and put it on top of one of mine. Damn it felt so nice and warm.

"You use any lube?" Trevor asked.

"If I've got something I do," I said.

He got up and his boner bounced around as he went to his dresser and got a tube of lube. He opened it and squirted a little on his fingers. And then he surprised me. He reached over and lubed up my cock.

I almost came when his hand touched it. He lubed it up and then lubed his own and we sat back down. That was the first time anyone had ever touched my cock besides me.

Trevor put his feet up on the bed I was sitting on. Damn they looked so nice. I took my free hand and rubbed his left foot.

"Oh that feels nice," he said. "Put your feet up on my side."

I did and he began massaging my foot with his free hand too.

Damn this was the most sensual jack off I'd ever had. Here I was watching a beautiful boy with a perfect cock, gorgeous body and lovely feet and he was jacking off in front of me.

After a few minutes Trevor began to make a sound in his throat.

"Getting close,' he whispered.

I increased my speed and soon I got the feeling too.

Suddenly, Trevor made a grunting sound and cum shot out of his cock up onto his chest. The second squirt landed on his left tit. Then he shot three more squirts onto his belly.

He looked at me and grinned and I closed my eyes and began shooting cum. I squirted five times and the dribbled more onto my pubes. Then we both lay back breathing hard and grinning.

"Damn that was hot," he said.

"Fuck I came so hard my balls hurt," I replied.

Trevor laughed and got up and grabbed a used towel from the closet. He came over to me and wiped the cum off my chest and belly and then cleaned my cock off. He didn't seem to worry about it at all. Then he wiped his chest off and his cock and sat down across from me.

"We'll have to do that again," I said.

"No doubt. That was hot. I'm glad I found another foot guy," he said.

Our cocks were only partly hard and pretty red and I loved looking at his as his shrunk up.

Just then Manny walked in carrying his shoes and shirt. He was all flushed and he stopped and grinned when he saw us sitting there naked with red cocks.

"Bueno," he said. "Mucho bueno."

My face was pretty red when I walked into my room. Jason was sitting in his boxers and just put his phone down. He looked up and grinned at me.

"So you and Trevor beat off together?"

"Who said that?"

"Manny just sent me a text. He said you two were naked and had red limp cocks when he got to his room."

"That little shit."

"Hey it's cool. Manny and I were fucking while you guys jacked off. Actually I'm surprised Trevor didn't get you to go farther than that."

"What do you mean, go farther?"

"Micah, Trevor is gay. Manny and I are gay."
"So why? What? Holy shit, you guys think I'm gay?"

"Aren't you?"

"Fuck no. I've never had sex with a guy. Never. What I just did with Trevor is as far as I've ever gone with another guy."

"Why is that?"

"What? What do you mean why?"

"What I mean is that if you'd had the chance to have sex with a guy and no one found out... would you?"

Holy fuck. He was right. The only reason I 'd not had guy sex was because I was too chicken to try it."

"I'm really confused right now," I said.

"Micah I'm sorry. This must be hard to get your mind around. I got a feeling when we talked at first that you might not be straight."

"What did I do to give you that idea?"

"Oh the way you looked at me. The way you looked at my cock and you getting a boner in the shower kind of made me think you liked cock."

"Yeah, I can see how that might make you think I was gay."

"After we ate with Manny and Trevor they both had the same feeling. We weren't trying to trap you. We thought it was something you wanted to happen."

Damn could it have been that obvious?

"Are you serious that you've never had sex with a guy?" he asked.

"Never."

"Wow, you're 18 and a virgin. I guess the three of us were right, you need some guy to guy sex."

"You figured it out in that little time? Did Trevor and Manny see it right away too?"

"They noticed the way you looked them over."

"I had no idea it was that obvious," I said.

"It probably isn't to a straight guy."

"I suppose the meeting didn't change your minds."

He grinned.

"Getting a boner when I felt up Manny at the meeting kind of sealed the deal. It all made sense."

"So you and Manny and Trevor are all gay?"

He nodded. "There are more too. I know of one other who is gay and a couple who are bi. Word gets around among wrestlers."

"Shit I never heard of any gay wrestlers where I live."

"Maybe there are none. But I doubt that. There are more gay guys around than you think Micah. Most are just regular guys, and you'd never know until their lips were wrapped around your cock. Some are all glam and swishy. They give us all a bad name. But the majority is just regular guys who you'd never suspect. The only thing that they do differently is suck cock instead of eat pussy."

"I guess you're right but I just never thought there would be that many gays in a small group like a wrestling team."

"They say one out of ten is gay. I think more like one out of seven is gay. So if your wrestling team had twenty guys there would probably be at least two or maybe three gay wrestlers. The team here is about forty guys. Later there'll be about 55 guys. The upperclassmen haven't come back yet. The guys here now are mostly freshmen. So this wrestling team could have anywhere from four to maybe six or seven gay guys. Throw in a few bi-guys that like cock and pussy and you've got a bunch of guys who like cock.

"Well fuck me," I said.

He grinned.

"I hope to one day."

I laughed. Damn after all these years of hiding, I finally had my first experience and now I had an opportunity to do more. Holy cow.

His phone buzzed. He read the text and grinned.

"Trevor says, hi."

"Tell him thanks for the fun."

He sent the text. His phone buzzed again.

He read the text and held it up to me. I read it. "MORE TO CUM!"

We sat around talking for a while and then Jason yawned.

"I think I'll take a shower and then hit the bed," he said.

I nodded.

"Care to join me?"

I grinned. "Sure why not?"

We both stripped naked and didn't try to hide our interest in the other's junk. We wrapped towels around each of us and walked down the hall to the shower. We turned on two spigots and both stood under the water enjoying the feel of the warmth running over us. I squeezed some shampoo onto my hair and began washing it. I had my eyes closed and suddenly I felt something warm on my cock. I opened my eyes and Jason was on his knees with my cock in his mouth.

"Holy shit!" I yelped.

He began laughing and stood up.

"Sorry," he said.

"No, it's all right, you just scared the shit out of me."

"So you didn't mind that I did that?"

I grinned. "No actually it felt pretty damn nice."

"No one's ever done that before?"

"Only in my dreams," I said.

He looked around and checked to see if anyone had come in.

"Watch the door," he said dropping to his knees.

I stood so I could see the door and Jason took my cock and put it in his mouth. I began getting hard immediately and he knew just what to do to make be harder and harder. His tongue was swirling around my dick head and he sucked it down his throat so far I didn't think it was possible. Then he took it out and sucked on my balls and licked my sack.

Damn I was in heaven.

Jason put my cock back in his mouth and took it deeply again and again and that really got me close to the end. I felt my cock begin to tingle.

"Jason I'm about to cum," I said urgently.

He nodded and went deep again.

"Jason, I'm not kidding, it's cumming."

I couldn't hold it back any longer. The first squirt actually made my balls hurt. Then I squirted four or five more times and he slurped it all down his throat. My knees began shaking and I had to grab the shower faucets to keep upright.

"Holy shit," I gasped.

He took my cock from his mouth and grinned up at me.

"How was that?" he said.

"Damn that was great."

"So now you can add blow job to the list of things you need to do."

I nodded.

"Damn I got a cherry," he said very proudly.

He stood up and I looked down at his cock. Damn! It was standing up like a soldier and it was a beauty. I reached for it.

"Let's dry off and finish up in our room. We've been pretty lucky not to get caught as it is."

I agreed and we both dried off and hurried back to our room. Jason locked the door and dropped his towel. His dick looked delicious.

I stepped up to him and reached out and took it in my hand. Oh man it felt so hard yet so soft and smooth. My hand was shaking. I sat on the bed and he stepped up in front of me. I looked up into his cute face and he smiled and nodded.

"Manny won't care?"

"Manny and I are very open in our relationship. Actually he urged me to do this."

I knew it was clean, I'd just seen him wash it, and so I opened my mouth and took about half of his cock into it. Damn it was just like I'd dreamt it would be. I licked his dick head with my tongue and began working more into my mouth. The head felt so smooth, like silk and the shaft was hard yet soft to the touch. I got about 2/3 in and gagged.

"Take it slow Micah, we're not in any hurry," he said.

"Lay down," I said patting the bed.

Jason lay on the bed and I got down next to him and put his cock back in my mouth. I sucked on it and enjoyed every minute. Then I sucked on his balls and licked his sack like he'd done to me. Jason had his hands in my hair and was rubbing my ears and hair.

I kept working his dick deeper into my mouth and soon had nearly the whole thing swallowed.

"Oh yeah, you're doing well," he whispered. "I'm getting close Micah."

I sucked him deeply another time and he began to pant.

"I'm close Micah if you don't want to get a mouthful take it out now."

I wasn't sure if I wanted him to cum in my mouth or not. But I'd waited for a long time to suck a cock and I wasn't going to miss one part of it, so I went deep again and felt his cock twitch. Then I tasted his cum shooting out into my mouth.

I'd licked up my own cum before so I knew what to expect. Jason's cum was great and there was a lot of it. He squirted hard several times and then his dick oozed more for a while. Finally he pulled his cock from my lips.

"Damn it's so sensitive, I can't take any more," he said breathlessly.

I lay down by him and looked into his pretty eyes. Damn he was a cute guy. He smiled at me.

"So?"

"It was everything I hoped it would be and ten times more."

"That was your first time?"

I nodded.

He leaned forward and kissed me lightly on the lips.

"Then I feel special for being your first."

"Thanks, Jason. Damn, I think I really lucked out getting you for a roommate."

"We've got two weeks Micah. We've got a lot more stuff to try."

Damn. I hit the jackpot.

Chapter Three

My phone began playing the theme from Rocky at 6:30 AM. I grabbed it and turned off the alarm. Jason groaned and I looked across the gap between our beds and saw him lying on his back, naked with a semi-boner. My cock began to grow immediately.

"What time is it?" he asked.

"It's 6:30. We have wrestling training at 7 o'clock," I said.

"Oh, fuck I hate early practices. I'm tired and I have a partial boner," he said.

Then he looked at me and grinned.

"You look like you've got a boner too. Do you think we have time?"

"We'll make time," I said.

I stepped across to his bed and took his cock in my hand. I began to bend down to suck it when he stopped me. He motioned for me to turn to the end of the bed and I got it right away.

I lay at his cock with mine at his face. I felt his mouth go over mine and damn it felt good. I took his in my mouth and began sucking him. In no time we were rubbing each other's butt cheeks and sucking on each other's nuts. Jason took my cock all the way down his throat and I knew the next time he did that it would be the end for me.

"I'm close," I said.

"Me too, go deep."

I went as deep as I could and felt his cock twitch. I could feel the warm cum shooting into my throat so I slid back and sucked on his dick head so I could taste it. My cock began shooting at the same time and I felt his tongue lapping at my slit. We sucked each other until we had no more cum.

Then we sat up and grinned at each other.

"Damn what a way to start the day," I said.

"Let's go brush our teeth," he said, "It wouldn't be a good idea to talk to the coach with cum breath."

We slipped on our boxers and sprinted to the bathroom and brushed our teeth standing side-by-side in front of the sinks. I looked at Jason in the mirror and marveled at how cute he was and how lucky I had been to find him. He looked at me and grinned.

"What?"

"Nothing. I just was thinking how damn adorable you are."

"Adorable and with a cock that won't quit," he said giggling.

"That too."

We hurried back to our room and put on shorts and a tee shirt each. We put on socks and our running shoes because we already knew what was coming.

The Science Building was three blocks away so we ran. When we got there the rest of the wrestlers were there and the coach was talking to them. He looked at us and at his watch.

"Have an appointment this morning?"

"No coach, sorry, we just got up a little late," I said.

I heard a throat clear and turned to see Trevor and Manny grinning. Manny put his hand up to his mouth like it was holding a dick and made a sucking motion. Jason and I grinned.

"Okay gentlemen, today is a day for conditioning. I wrestler who isn't in good condition wears out and gets pinned. The stairs here go to the 4th floor. When you get to the top you'll run down the hall to the other end of the building and find another stairs just like them You'll run down to this level, and across the hallway to here and up the stairs again... five times. Then, one more time at a walk to cool down. Any questions?"

I looked at Jason and he made a face.

"Okay gentlemen, hit it."

Most of us hadn't worked out since wrestling season ended in March. By the time we got to the fourth floor many were already breathing hard. Five laps later we all were bathed in sweat and dragging ass. Jason and I stayed together. When we started our walking round we were about dead.

"Why are we doing this to ourselves?" Trevor said walking up behind us.

"For the glory of sport," I said.

"Oh thanks I forgot."

"Fuck me," Manny said. "I think my balls dropped off the third time up the stairs."

"Well go find them, I like sucking on them," Jason said.

We drug our butts to the end and the coach congratulated us on a job well done. He reminded us that we had another session at 4PM. There were a lot of groans.

The four of us walked slowly back to the dorm.

"Pew, I need a shower," Manny said.

"You sure do you stinky little Mexican," Jason said.

Manny grabbed him and pulled on his cock.

"Stop that. I'll give you fifteen minutes to stop that!"

"How about a group shower?" Trevor said.

"What about the others?"

"Fuck them if they can't take a joke."

We went to our room and stripped down naked. It was the first time I'd seen Manny and he was as cute naked as I expected him to be. He was really a tiny little shit. His skin was dark like a real good tan and he had a thick black bush over a nice sized un-circumcised cock. His feet were so tiny I couldn't believe them.

"Damn Manny what size feet do you have?"

"They're 7 ½ but I wear a size 8 shoe."

"Shit mine were size 7 ½ when I was nine," I said.

"Wait till you see that little brown sausage hard," Jason said.

I grinned. I hoped it would be real soon.

Since there were no other guys on our floor in the area we all just walked naked to the shower carrying our towels. We turned on all of the spigots and enjoyed the water running over us. We were beat after the workout at the science building.

"Damn I thought I was gonna puke the last time we had to run up those stairs," Trevor said.

"My ass was dragging too," I said.

Manny looked around behind me and smiled.

"It looks okay now," he said grinning.

"Maybe a little massage would help," I said.

Manny moved behind me and began squeezing my butt cheeks. Jason and Trevor got close to each other and began playing with their cocks. I began boning up feeling Manny's hands on me and watching those two beauties getting hard.

Suddenly Manny reached around and grabbed my cock and began jacking me off. Trevor dropped to his knees and took Jason's cock into his mouth.

I felt something in my butt cheeks and realized Manny was up against me and his cock was pushing between my cheeks. It felt huge.

"Damn, Manny, what you got in there?" I said.

"My big *enchilada*," he said grinning.

I turned and my mouth dropped open. Manny's little brown cock was standing up at a 45-degree angle from his little flat belly. The head was peeking out of the foreskin and the damn thing looked like it was at least seven inches long! It had a curve up toward his belly and his balls hung down like a couple of hen's eggs. The kid was hung like the Hulk!

"Fuck me," I said. "How big is that thing?"

"Seven and one quarter inch," Jason said.

I laughed. Leave it to Jason to be precise on dick measurements.

"Taste it," Manny said.

I didn't have to be asked twice. I dropped to my knees and pulled the big thing down so I could get the head in my mouth. I took it in my hand and skinned it back and his dick head slid out of the foreskin. It was pink and lovely. I licked it and he moaned.

"Suck it Micah," he said.

I took it in my mouth and got less than half in. It was huge and there was no way I'd ever get it in all the way. I sucked on it and licked the head and Manny seemed to like it. He was moaning and speaking Spanish.

Trevor began laughing.

"Manny reverts to Spanish when he's getting pleasured," he said.

"I should be speaking it too then," I said.

I licked Manny's balls. Damn they were huge. I knew mine were pretty good sized by the ones I'd seen in locker rooms while wrestling but his were the biggest I'd ever seen.

"You like my *cojones*?" He asked.

"If that means balls, you damn right I like them."

"Let me suck your *pene*," he said.

I figured that meant penis so I got up and he knelt down. I looked and Jason was now sucking Trevor too.

Manny took my cock in his hand and looked it over.

"*Grande,*" he said.

He opened his mouth and took the damn thing all the way to my pubes. I could feel his throat constricting on the head and it felt like he was milking it. I damn near fell down.

"Holy fuck Manny," I gasped.

Jason began laughing.

"That little taco-bender can sure suck a cock hey?"

"Fuck I thought it was coming off my body," I said.

Manny sucked me and it was amazing. I didn't want to cum so I could keep this going. I looked at Trevor and winked.

"How about we switch again so I can taste Trevor's cock?" I said.

We shifted around and I had the beautiful cock of one of the most handsome boys I'd ever met in my mouth. It wasn't as big as Manny's but it was perfect for sucking.

I licked Trevor's sack and sucked each of his balls into my mouth. He leaned his head back and gasped.

"You better get on it, I'm about to cum," he said urgently.

I pulled his cock down and just got the head into my mouth when he shot the first squirt. I sucked on his dick head while he filled my mouth with hot cum. I didn't even think about not swallowing it. He stopped cumming and pulled away from me.

"Mine gets so sensitive when I cum. I can't stand it," he said.

Manny was sucking Jason and suddenly he yelled, *"Olay!"*

I could see him swallowing and Jason had his eyes closed and was filling Manny's mouth with cum. Trevor and I stood there side-by-side watching them and he was fondling my cock.

"Okay who wants to get Manny and Micah off?" he asked.

"I'll do Manny," Jason said.

"I guess you get me," Trevor said dropping to his knees.

"Damn just my luck."

He pinched my cock.

Then he took it in his mouth and worked it until I knew I was there.

"I'm close Trev."

He went deep on it and I began cumming. He slid back to the tip and sucked on it and nearly drove me wild. I finally stopped oozing and he licked the slit and let it drop.

"Damn that was nice," I said.

He stood up and we watched Jason sucking Manny. He was getting damn near the whole thing in his mouth. Suddenly Manny clenched his cute little butt cheeks together and grabbed Jason's head and Jason started swallowing. He had a hard time keeping up and some cum leaked out of his mouth and down his chin. Manny finally stopped cumming and pulled his cock from Jason's lips.

He pulled Jason up and then licked his own cum off his chin. He turned and grinned at us.

"Anyone ready for breakfast?"

We finished up washing and dried off. They wore their towels up to their room and Jason and I went to ours and dressed in shorts and tees and flip-flops. We met Manny and Trevor similarly dressed in the lobby and walked to the food center and had our breakfast.

"So what shall we do the rest of the day?"

"We've got more "conditioning" at 4 o'clock," I said.

"He won't make us run again will he?"

"Damn I hope not. I'm all run out for the day," Jason said.

"Well we could go down to the beach for a while," Trevor said.

"I didn't know there was a beach," I said.

"There's a nice lake about three miles out of town. They hauled in a bunch of sand and made a pretty nice swimming beach. We could go there and swim and who-knows-what?"

Jason and Manny grinned.

"I like who-knows-what," Manny said.

Chapter Four

We'd all brought swimming suits because there was a pool at the college that we could use. Trevor drove his car and we took along a couple of blankets and a football. When we got to the beach there were several people swimming and some just sunning themselves. We saw a couple more wrestlers that we recognized from the camp.

"Let's see if they want to play some touch football," Trevor suggested.

We walked over to the guys who were in the water. Trevor asked them if they wanted to play and they said they did. We found out one was named Chris and the other Dave. Chris was a 170-pound weight class guy and Dave wrestled at 165. They were both well built and not bad looking.

We ended up with Chris, Manny and me against the other three. We had a lot of fun running and ended up doing more tackling than touching. Several times the person who caught a pass ended up getting shoved into the lake, which caused a lot of laughter.

They had the ball and Jason made a run and Manny brought him down. They rolled around in the sand and suddenly Jason's swimming suit was around his ankles. Manny had pants'd him. Jason kicked his swimming suit off his feet and jumped up. Manny took off running and laughing like crazy.

"You little Mexican turd," Jason said as he ran bare-ass after Manny. They ended up in the water and after a fight that went under water many times Jason emerged carrying Manny's swimming suit. We laughed our butts off.

Manny came out of the water and he had a giant boner. Chris and Dave almost pooped.

"Now see what you did to me," he said to Jason who was rolling on the sand laughing.

"Sorry *muchacho*," Jason said.

"You have to make up for it. Follow me."

Manny marched off down toward a little patch of woods and Jason followed him. They were both as naked as the day they were born. They disappeared into the woods.

"What the hell?" Chris said.

"It looks like the game is over," I said.

"What're they doing?" Dave asked.

Trevor shrugged. He made a gesture with his hips that looked like fucking and laughed.

"No shit?"

"I think they do that a lot," Trevor said.

"I'll be damned."

We stood there a while and here came the two little shits back. Jason was walking kind of bow-legged and Manny was grinning from ear-to-ear.

"Anyone else want to mess with *"El Toro"*?"

"El Toro? The bull?"

Manny grabbed his crotch and shook it.

"Fuck with the bull... you get the horn."

Jason just grinned.

THE AFTERNOON practice was at the gym so we didn't think we'd be running again. All of us had sore legs from the workout in the morning. We did have to take a couple of laps around the gym to get warmed up and then we worked on weights. We paired up so we could spot for each other. Of course Jason and Manny paired up because they were the same weight class. There were two others at 145#'s so Trevor and I got split up. One was a kid named Cody who paired up with me. He was not bad looking and had a nice body. Of course everyone there had a nice body.

Trevor paired up with a kid named Sam who was short and stocky with dark hair and really hairy legs.

We wrestled for a while and then Cody sat on the bench to do bench presses. I stood behind him and spotted in case he got in trouble. I noticed he was back quite far on the bench but didn't think much of it. He did a few reps and then we added weights. He lay back down again and I straddled his head and spotted him.

I looked down and he was looking up the leg of my shorts. I was wearing my boxers under them and I suppose the boxers were open at the bottom. He was looking at my cock and balls and seemed to be pretty interested in them.

I looked at his crotch. Damn he had a semi-boner.

"Maybe you want to switch?" I said.

He looked a little embarrassed.

"Yeah, let's switch," he said.

I made a point of looking at his boner when he got up so he knew I saw it. He kind of grinned and I lay down on the bench.

He hitched up his shorts so they were up high on his hips and I looked and there his cock was hanging down the left leg of them. I grinned and he looked at me and winked.

I did my reps and we worked on some other weights. Then we trotted off to the bathroom for a piss break.

We walked in and up to the urinal. I pulled my shorts down over my ass cheeks and hauled out my semi-hard cock. He pulled the front of his shorts down and hauled his out too. We both just stood there looking at the other's cock.

"Damn you've got a thick one," he said.

His was longer than mine but skinnier.

"How long is that?" I asked.

"Almost eight inches," he said.

"No way. Damn."

He grinned. Then he took his dick head in his hand and stretched his cock out and the damn thing was really long.

We stood there and we both knew we wanted to touch the other's cock. I finally motioned to a stall with my head.

We walked in and shut the door.

"Stand on the seat," he said. "That way if someone comes in they'll only see one set of feet."

Hmm, he'd done this before.

I stepped up on the seat and he pulled my shorts down and took hold of my cock.

"Oh man that's nice," he said as he opened his mouth and started sucking me.

He definitely had sucked a cock before. He knew just what to do to make it feel good. He was working it over and rubbing my balls with his free hand and then he slid his finger up my ass crack and began rubbing my asshole!

Damn I'd not had that done before and it really felt good. In fact it felt so good I got the feeling.

"I'm about to cum," I whispered.

He nodded and shoved his finger into my ass deeper. I erupted with a hard cum that made my toes curl. He made a surprised little yelp but didn't lose a drop of cum. I was panting and suddenly we heard a door open.

"Micah, you in here?"

It was Jason.

"Um yeah, I'm just finishing up."

"Coach wants you to scrimmage with Trevor."

"Okay I'll be right there."

Cody wiped his mouth off and shrugged his shoulders.

"I'll owe you one," I said.

"Okay thanks that was fun."

I went back to wrestle. While Trevor and I were rolling around on the mat I saw Cody sneak back in and join the others. We went off the mat and as we were walking back to the middle Trevor grinned at me.

"With him?"

I smiled.

"You fucker."

The four of us were walking back to the dorm.

"So how big is his cock?" Jason asked.

"It's long, he said eight inches," I replied.

"Damn did you suck him?"

"No dildo head, some dope interrupted me just when I was about to get to suck him."

"Soreee."

"I did get a hell of a good blow job though."

"You fucker, you owe all of us one then," Manny said.

"How do you figure?"

"That's the rules," he said.

"Yup, the rule is if one of the Four Amigos gets head without the others he is required to give the others head when demanded."

We all were laughing.

"So I have to blow all three of you?"

"It's the law," Manny said.

"Can it wait until after dinner? I'm really hungry."

"Okay but as soon as we finish dinner we all get a blow job."

"Okey-dokey," I said. Damn that sounded like a deal to me.

WE HAD a lot of fun at dinner. I was getting to like these guys as good friends as well as sex partners. They were really good guys... who happened to like cock.

We got back to the dorm and Trevor and Manny wanted us to come up to their room. Manny and Jason had some game they wanted to play so I went along with it.

"So first we have to all get naked," Manny said.

Well I liked that idea. So we all took off our clothes and sat two on each bed with a little table in between the beds. Manny got a little box out with a spinner on top of it. There were different sections on the box of different colors and each had something written in it.

I looked at the box. One little section was labeled "Suck cock", the next said "Lick Ass", then there was "Suck Balls", "French Kiss", "Suck any body part as requested" and "Fuck". It had been a spinner for some other game and someone had made little paper signs that said these things and taped them over the original words.

Holy shit, I had only done a couple of those things.

"Okay since Micah is the visiting lady, he spins first," Jason said smirking.

I spun the spinner. It stopped on "Lick Ass".

"Oh goodie," I said. "Who gets to do it?"

"You do dumb ass. You have to lick one of our butt cracks. Jeez what a dope," Manny said.

I reached over and gave him a titty twister and he yelped and ducked away.

"How do we decide who I lick?"

"Spin the spinner… duh."

I reached over to grab him again but he was too quick. He hopped up on the back of the bed like a little brown monkey. I spun the spinner and it stopped on Manny, wouldn't you know?

"Bueno," he said. He got up on the bed and bent over and spread his butt cheeks. Damn, there was his little pink asshole looking me right in the face. I knew it was clean because we'd all just showered an hour ago.

Trevor and Jason were slowly stroking their cocks watching. I got up and leaned in and stuck my tongue on his hole. It was smooth and slick and damn erotic. I began licking up from his balls to the top of his butt crack and he moaned and shivered.

"Oh yeah Mikey, you do that good."

I licked his balls a little and then sat down.

"Okay who's next?" I asked.

Manny jumped up.

"I'll go next," he said. His brown boner was standing up and looked damn nice.

He spun the spinner and it landed on "Fuck".

"Okie dokey," he said grinning. "Now who shall I fuck?"

He spun the spinner and I held my breath. I'd never done this and never even seen it done so I was hoping he'd land on someone else. It landed on Jason.

He got a big smile on his face. He was hoping to be the one.

Manny grabbed a box from his dresser and opened it. There must have been fifty condoms in it.

"Holy shit, are you prepared." I said.

"Always," he said digging in the box. He pulled out one that said Magnum on the package.

"I need these extra-large ones for my huge boner," he said ripping the package open. I watched fascinated as he rolled it down his cock and then got a little tube of lube and lubed it up. Jason got on his hands and knees and Manny lubed up his asshole. Jason closed his eyes and I knew he was enjoying it.

Manny got behind him on his knees too and took his cock in his hand and guided it into Jason's hole. Jason moaned at first but soon it looked like Manny was in and Jason began acting like he was having a great time. Manny's little brown ass was going like a damn bunny.

I looked over at Trevor and he was watching intently. His cock was wet on the end and I leaned down and licked it off. He looked at me and smiled.

I guess it took six or seven minutes and then Manny began grunting and he slammed into Jason and held it there. Jason closed his eyes and sighed.

"I can feel it Manny," he said.

Manny pulled out and his cock was still huge but not as hard as before. The condom was about a quarter full of cum. He pulled it off and held up the cum for Trevor and me to see.

"*Bueno*," he said nodding.

"Damn impressive," I said.

He tied a knot in the condom and tossed it into the wastebasket. Then he wiped his dick off and Jason's ass off with a used towel.

"Who's next?

Jason took a spin. It landed on "French Kiss." He grinned and spun again and it stopped on Trevor.

"Oh yay," he said.

He got up and climbed up on Trevor's lap. He put his legs on the sides of Trevor and sat on his hard cock. They wrapped their arms around each other and began kissing. My cock was so hard it hurt.

Manny and I both were leaking like mad as we watched them making out. We could see their mouths open and tongues darting in and out. They went at it for many minutes and then Jason let up and stood up. He leaned down and pecked Trevor on the nose. When he stepped away he stumbled.

"Whooie, that was pretty intense," he said. "Damn, he kisses well."

Trevor looked a little dazed. His cock was actually throbbing with his heartbeat.

"Your turn Trev," Manny said.

Trevor spun the spinner. It stopped on "Fuck".

He grinned and looked at all of us. Then he spun again and it stopped on me.

I must have looked scared.

"You've never fucked before have you?" he asked.

I shook my head.

"This is all new to me. I mean I've thought of doing this for years but until we got here to camp, it's all just been a dream and a lot of jacking off."

"I can re-spin. You don't have to do it if you don't want to."

"I'll do it," I said quickly.

"Are you sure Micah?"

If I was going to lose my virginity I sure as hell couldn't find a more beautiful guy than Trevor to do it with.

"Just go slow," I said.

Manny and Jason scooted together to watch. They had their arms around each other and were playing with each other's cocks.

Trevor chose a condom and rolled it down his cock. I was glad it was Trevor and not Manny who was fucking me. Trevor had a beautiful cock and it looked like it would hurt a lot less than that big thing hanging from Manny's crotch.

"Want me on my knees?" I asked.

"Lay on your back," he said. He smiled at me.

I lay on the bed and he pulled me to the end so my ass was right at the end of the mattress. He got a pillow and I lifted up and he put it under my ass. Then he had me lift my legs.

He stood there smiling.

"You've got a nice ass," he said quietly.

Then he leaned down and licked my asshole. I didn't expect that. I guess I got a bonus.

He licked me and it felt amazing. Then he put some lube on his finger and slid it into my hole.

"I'll loosen you up so it won't hurt so much," he said.

I nodded that I understood. I was so fucking nervous I didn't know if I could talk.

He worked my hole and then put in another finger. My ass was feeling pretty nice. His fingers felt great. I couldn't imagine how good his cock would feel. Then he got in close and I could feel his dick head pushing against my hole.

It felt like a damn log. I closed my eyes and held my breath and suddenly it slid in. He stopped and let me get used to it.

"Are you okay? I can take it out," he said.

My ass hurt but it wasn't as bad as I'd expected. I opened my eyes and looked up at this most beautiful boy and smiled.

"Go ahead," I whispered.

Trevor worked his beautiful cock into me and his balls were slapping against my ass. He fucked me slowly and gently. The pain went away and a beautiful feeling took over. I could feel his cock sliding through my ass and it felt amazing.

I wanted him to keep doing it so I wrapped my legs around him.

"See, he likes it," Manny said.

"Good huh?" Jason giggled.

"Oh fuck," I said.

Trevor increased his speed and began to get a look on his beautiful face. I knew he was close. Manny reached over and took my cock in his hand and began jacking me. He watched Trevor and when he saw him shudder he knew he was cumming and he jacked me real fast and I my cock shot cum out clear up onto my face. I could feel Trevor's cock throbbing inside me and mine was squirting cum all over the place. Trevor finally stopped cumming and fell forward onto me. I wrapped my arms around him and we kissed, deeply.

"Oh man," Jason said quietly.

Trevor and I lay there panting. I could feel the heat from his body and his heart beating. He was sweating and looked down at me.

"That was beautiful," I said.

"I'm glad you liked it. I'm honored to be your first," he said.

He kissed me again and got up.

Manny and Jason sat looking amazed.

"That was about the sexiest thing I've ever seen," Jason said.

"It was beautiful," Manny added.

Trevor's cock was half soft and the condom was dangling off the end. He pulled it off and held it up. It was half full.

"Damn you made me cum a hell of a lot," he said.

I looked at him and then at myself. We were both covered with cum.

"I think we need a shower," I said.

He held out his hand and helped me up from the bed.

"Back in a jiffy," I said to the boys.

"Don't do anything we wouldn't do," Trevor added.

He and I each grabbed a towel and walked hand-in-hand to the shower. It felt right and we didn't care if anyone saw us or not.

Chapter Five

Early practice was running at the Science Building again the next day. I can't say it was any easier but it seemed to go by faster. I was running up the stairs when I heard someone say my name. I turned and it was Cody.

"How's it hangin'?" he asked.

I grinned.

"Pretty soft and loose right now."

"I hope you'll keep what we did to yourself," he said.

"Don't worry I'm not going to broadcast it," I said.

"I'm just, well, I have a girlfriend and if she ever got wind of that she'd kill me."

"So you play on both teams," I said.

Another kid caught up to us and passed us.

"I like both. I figure what the hell? I get twice the chance for some sex if I do it both ways."

"Good thinking," I said.

"There's a couple more bi-guys on the team," he said.

"Really? How do you know?"

"We fooled around last year at a summer wrestling camp."

"Anyone I know?"

"I think you met them. Chris and Dave are their names. They wrestle in the 165 range."

"We met them at the lake."

"Yeah, those guys. I bet if you'd have come a bit later they'd have been in the bushes fucking," he said.

Damn. I was beginning to think everyone on the wrestling squad liked cock.

"Are there any more?"

"I'm not sure. Wrestlers get a lot of body contact with other guy's cocks and stuff. I think they kind of get comfortable with another guy holding them and having their hands where most guys never have some other guy's hands. Some decide they like it and take it farther."

"There are a lot of naked guys around at the weigh-ins and the locker rooms," I said.

He nodded.

"Lots of group showers and helping each other rub out muscle aches. A lot of schools have saunas for the wrestlers. There are a bunch of chances for it."

"Damn I never figured it that way but I think you're right."

We were at the top floor and started down the hall. There was a men's restroom on the right and I motioned toward it. Cody grinned and we slipped inside.

"I owe you one," I said.

We got into a stall and he stood on the toilet. I pulled his shorts down and his cock was about half hard. Damn it was a long one. I grabbed it and started jacking him and it boned up real fast. It was not real thick but the longest one I'd ever seen.

"Damn," I said.

I took it in my hand and opened my mouth and put it in. It was a little salty from him sweating but it was still very nice. He gasped as I took about half of it. I played with his balls and sucked him and jacked the lower half.

He held my head between his hands and it didn't take long and I felt him twitching in my mouth. I tasted his cum as it shot out onto my tongue.

"Ahh, ahh, ahh," he said quiet loudly.

"Shh, jeez they'll hear you."

He laughed.

"Sorry, damn that felt good."

He pulled up his shorts and we grinned at each other.

"There, debt paid," I said.

"And thank you very much," he said.

We peeked out of the door and it was clear so we stepped out and ran down the hall. When we got to the first floor everyone was sitting or walking slowly cooling off. Manny and Jason looked at me and they knew right away.

"You fucker," Jason mouthed.

I just grinned.

"**SO YOU** just took a little break in running this morning and sucked that kid's dick?" Jason asked while we ate breakfast.

"That would be true," I said.

"Fucker!"

"Why thank you," I said.

"Now you have to suck all of us," Manny said.

"Huh? I thought I had to do that if I got sucked."

"And if you sucked someone else… it's the law."

We all laughed and Manny grinned and nodded his head.

"My lower legs are sore as hell from all the running. How about after breakfast we go to the gym and have a sauna?"

They all were grinning when I suggested that. We finished up our breakfast and walked over to the gym. There were a couple of the guys playing basketball. We watched for a minute and it was obvious why they were wrestlers. They were terrible basketball players.

We walked down the hall to the training room and stripped off our clothes. We got a towel from a pile of them next to the hallway and walked to the sauna. I was last and admired the three perfect butts in front of me. Trevor's was tight and obviously very muscular. Jason's was round and a perfect bubble butt and Manny's was brown and made my mouth water.

We walked into the sauna and there sat Chris and Dave, the guys from the lake. They were sitting right next to each other and both hurriedly grabbed a towel and put it on their laps.

It was obvious that we'd caught them fucking around. They both had big bulges in their towel.

"Hey, what's up?" Trevor said.

"Other than your dicks," Jason said quietly to me.

"Oh um, not much. We were sore so we thought a little heat would help," Chris said.

Their faces were bright red.

We took our towels off and lay them on the benches and sat down. Manny and Jason were across from them and Trevor and I sat to the left of them on the same side. It was obvious they were checking out our cocks.

"So you guys all live in the same dorm?" Dave asked.

"Yeah, he and I share," Jason nodded to me. "And Trev and Manny share a room."

"We do too but in that dorm next to the food place."

There was a kind of pregnant silence for a bit.

"Whew, it's warm in here," Jason said laying back so his cock was real obvious.

"That's why they call it a sauna, dumb ass," Manny said.

"Fuck you, you Mexican beaner," Jason quipped.

Manny reached over and grabbed Jason's cock and twisted it. Jason let out a yelp and they were off the bench and on the floor wrestling. We all were laughing and cheering as they rolled around on the floor grabbing each other's cocks and balls. Manny had Jason down on his back and his cute little ass was in the air with his asshole showing. I saw Chris reach under his towel and pull on his dick.

I nodded to Trevor and grinned. He nodded slightly and leaned back and I reached over nonchalantly and began stroking him. Dave saw that and I thought he was going to shit.

He elbowed Chris and they both watched as I got Trevor hard. Of course my cock was hardening up at the same time.

Jason and Manny had quieted down and I looked down and they were head to toe sucking each other off.

Chris saw that and I thought he'd have a heart attack.

"Um, um," he said.

"We're all good friends," I said.

I leaned over and took Trevor's cock in my mouth and began sucking him.

"Holy fuck," Dave said quietly.

They sat and watched for a minute and then they tossed their towels aside and began playing with each other's cocks. I looked up at Trevor and we got up and Trevor sat down next to Chris and I sat next to Dave and we took hold of their cocks and played with them.

"We're not gay," he said.

"That's okay, we're equal opportunity cock suckers, just lean back and enjoy," I said.

Trevor and I began sucking them off and Manny and Jason got up and stood on the bench, Manny by Chris and Jason by Dave. Their cocks were right in their faces. They both looked for a second or two and then they grabbed the cock next to them and began sucking it. Damn a six-way.

In the next fifteen minutes or so we moved around so everyone got a taste of all the cocks in the room. It was hot as hell and we were all sweating and slippery. There were moans and groans and lots of slurping. It was pretty damn exciting for a guy like me who'd never even touched another guy's cock until a few days ago.

We were going at it and suddenly the door opened. One of the smaller kids who wrestled below Jason and Manny walked in. He stopped, his mouth dropped open and he turned around and was gone.

"Oops," Jason said.

"I hope he doesn't tell anyone," Dave said.

"I doubt it. He just looked surprised. He didn't look disgusted."

"I'll go see," Manny said jumping up and running out the door, naked and with a boner.

"Fucking Manny, he could talk anyone into fucking with him," Jason said.

We all went back to the cock in hand and a few minutes later here came Manny… and the kid.

"Guys, this is Paul," he said.

"Hi Paul," we all said.

"Come and join us."

Paul was even smaller than Jason. He wrestled at the lowest weight. He looked like he was about fourteen but I asked him and he was nearly nineteen. There were a lot of wrestlers like that who dieted all the years they should have been growing and ended up being way behind the growth curve.

Paul had a towel around his tiny body and Manny helped him take it off. He had a boner and it was pretty damn nice for such a little guy. It was about five inches and about the size of a good bratwurst. He had small balls and a teeny little thin pubic bush.

"Come over," Trevor said.

We moved apart and Paul got in the middle of us. He looked scared to death.

"If you don't want to do this, it's okay," I said.

"I do but I've never done it before," he said with an almost child-like voice.

"Then lay back and let us make you feel good," Manny said.

The six of us went to work. Jason began kissing Paul's ears and face. Trevor sucked on his left nipple and Dave sucked his right one. I lifted his cute little feet and sucked his toes and licked his soles. Chris got between his legs and licked his nuts and Manny took his cock in his mouth.

The kid looked like he was going to have a stroke. He closed his eyes and sighed. Jason began kissing him on the lips and he kissed back passionately. He reached over and took Trevor's cock in one hand and Dave's in the other. Chris lifted up his nuts and licked his ass crack.

Suddenly, he began making a squeaking sound and Manny made a moaning noise. I could see him holding his mouth on Paul's cock head.

Paul thrashed around and then he stopped and lay still panting. Manny opened up his mouth and showed us his tongue. He had a big gob of thick cum on it. He showed us and then closed his mouth and swallowed it.

We all sat back and looked down at Paul.

"Are you okay?" Jason asked.

"Am I in heaven?"

We all laughed. "No you're in the sauna," Manny said.

"Holy crap. I've thought about kissing a guy for years. I've thought about having my nipples sucked and my balls sucked and my toes sucked. I've wanted to get my cock sucked for as long as I knew it was good for something but peeing. But I never thought I'd have all it done at once. You guys damn near killed me!"

Damn he was a cute little guy. We all smiled at him and helped him up.

"Well now you know. Any time you want to play just ask," Jason said.

"Really? You'd let me… um touch you guys cocks?"

Manny moved in close. His big brown cock was standing up and had precum on the tip.

"Go ahead," he said.

Paul reached out carefully like he was afraid it would bite him. He wrapped his hand around it and jacked it a little. Precum oozed out of the end. He looked up at Manny and Manny nodded.

"You guys won't tell will you?" he said looking around.

"Our little secret Paul," I said.

Paul leaned forward and licked it off. He closed his eyes and we could tell he liked it. He smiled.

"It's good," he said.

"Try some more," Trevor said. His cock was all shiny with precum.

Paul did us all. He licked precum off all our cocks and took them in his mouth. By now he was hard again so Chris dropped to his knees and began sucking him. I went down on Jason, Manny took Dave, Trevor sucked me and in a short time we all were cumming or had cummed.

There were a lot of limp red dicks hanging.

"Wow, it's hot in here," Jason said.

Manny looked at me.

"You know, I only love Jason for his cock, not his brains."

"Fuck you Manny," Jason said.

"Later, it's too hot in here."

We all laughed and walked down the hall to the showers. Little Paul acted like he was in a dream. He had a boner again by the time we got there so I dropped down and sucked him off again. He came but not much. The poor little guy's balls were empty.

We all were dressed and walking out when Paul stopped and said, "So we can do this again sometime?"

"Don't worry Paulie, we'll let you know the next time we decide on an orgy."

"Any time little man," Trevor said. We all got each other's phone numbers so if something came up, we could gather the troops. It was time for a nap.

We watched the little guy walking down the street. He acted like he was in a dream.

After the 4 o'clock practice Trevor and Manny went downtown to a sporting goods store. Manny's wrestling shoes were done for and he needed some new ones so Trevor volunteered to take him shopping. Jason and I opted for a nap.

They weren't back by dinnertime so we figured they'd stopped for a pizza. Jason and I went to the food center to eat dinner. We'd just sat down when Paul came up carrying his tray.

"Can I sit with you guys?" he asked bashfully.

"Sure, grab a chair," I said.

"So how are you guys?" he asked.

"We're good Paulie. What did you do after the late practice?"

"I took a nap, I was beat," he said.

We laughed because that was the same for us.

"So how do you feel about the sauna today?" Jason asked.

"You mean how do I feel about what we did together?"

Jason nodded.

"I've known for long time that I was different. When my friends and I got a little older they'd show up at a sleepover or something with porn magazines and all get boners over girls with big tits and hairy pussies. I didn't even come close but had to pretend because I didn't want them to know. I did get boners sometimes because some of them got theirs out and stuff. So when I saw you guys all naked and doing that stuff I knew I wasn't the only one who was that way. But I was so shocked I ran."

"Good thing Manny doesn't give a shit what people think," I said.

"I about shit when I saw him running after me with that big cock of his but he was really nice and told me that if I wanted to join it was cool and if not it was cool too. I knew that was my chance to see if I was really... gay."

"And it's okay," I said.

"Yeah I guess so."

"Chris and Dave aren't gay. They're bisexual. They both have girlfriends. But there are guys who just like to have sex and it doesn't matter too much to them if it's with a guy or a girl."

"I was wondering about that. I had a good friend in high school that had a really pretty steady girlfriend. I walked in on him and another guy once in the shower and they were kissing. I turned around real quickly and left but it really surprised me."

"A few years ago, like when our parents or grandparents were our age, it was a big deal, but I think kids now don't mind if a friend is gay or straight or bi," I said.

"Well, put me in the gay column," he said grinning.

"You liked it?"

"Damn I'll never forget it," he said.

We ate our dinner and walked to the door.

"Which dorm are you in?" Jason asked.

He was in the one next door to us.

"Why don't you come over for a while?"

"And do what?"

"Whatever. Manny and Trevor should be back any time. Maybe we can think of something to pass the time," I said.

"Let's go," the little guy said smiling from ear-to-ear.

WHEN WE got back Jason ran upstairs to see if they were back. He called down and said to come up.

Paul and I walked up the stairs and I could see he had a boner already. I opened the door and there was Jason on the floor on his hands and knees and Manny was fucking him. Jason had Manny's underwear on his head like a hat.

I thought Paul was going to faint.

"What the hell is going on?" I said laughing.

"My ears were cold," Jason said mugging from the floor.

Paul's eyes got real big and he watched Manny's big cock going in and out of Jason's ass.

"I knew you could do that but I've never seen anything like that before. How the heck does something that big go in a little hole like that?"

"It stretches out Paul," Trevor said. He was sitting on the bed playing with his cock but still dressed.

"Come down and look," Manny said.

Paul got down on his hands and knees and watched as Manny fucked Jason. He looked from above and then from below. Jason's balls were swinging back and forth and his cock was only semi-hard.

"Why don't you have a boner?" Paul asked.

"It kind of hurts at first and my boner died," Jason said grinning. "Take hold of it and it'll come back to life."

Paul looked up at Trevor and me and we shrugged. He reached under Jason's belly and we could tell he was enjoying himself. Jason grinned at us and looked like he had a question. I knew he was asking if he should try to fuck Paul and I shrugged.

"Hey Paulie, when Manny's done with me, do you want to try it?"

"You mean me and you?"

"Yeah, you can fuck me or I'll fuck you. My dick, while glorious, isn't as huge as Manny's and would be a lot easier for you to take for the first time."

Paul looked at Trevor and me and I said, "No pressure. If you want to try it now is the time. If not it's fine."

He thought for a minute.

"When he's done I'll decide," he said.

Trevor and I took off our clothes and Paul saw that he was the only one dressed so he stripped too.

I looked at him closely since I really had too many cocks and balls to look at in the sauna. He was about five feet six inches tall and maybe weighed a hundred pounds or a bit more. He was skinny but had a cute little butt. His legs were nearly completely hairless and he had just a few wispy hairs under his arms. He got down and was looking under Jason at his cock and his little butt cheeks spread apart showing his cute pink little hole.

"Cute," Trevor said as he reached over and began stroking my cock.

"Adorable," I said. I leaned over and kissed Trevor. Damn I was getting to like this kid more and more.

Manny started making some kind of animal noise and suddenly he shoved into Jason and began speaking Spanish really fast. Jason began laughing and so did the rest of us.

Manny pulled out of Jason and held up the half full condom.

"*El Toro,*" he said, "I am like the bull."

Jason sat over on his bare ass on the floor and looked down at Paul's hard cock.

"Hey sailor, you've got a boner there, need a hand?"

"Huh?"

"Never mind. Did you decide if you want to get fucked or fuck?"

"If it hurts too much would you take it out?"

"Paul, I'm not going to rape you. If you don't like it, it's no problem. I'm sure Trevor or Micah will love my perfect boner in their ass."

Paul grinned.

"Okay, I want you to do it to me."

"Do what?"

Paul got red in the face.

"Fuck me," he said grinning.

"Okey dokey," Jason said springing up.

He got the condom box and found one he liked. He handed it to Paul and Paul just stood there looking at it."

"I need one too?"

"No dumb ass, roll it down my cock."

"Oh sorry," he said.

Trevor and I giggled watching the two little shits.

Paul's hands were shaking as he rolled the condom down Jason's cock. Then Jason had him lay on the bed on his back.

"Lift up your legs," he said.

Paul lifted his legs and Jason grinned when he saw his virgin butt hole.

"You've never had anything in there?"

Paul turned red.

"What? You *have* had something in there?"

"Well, when I was younger."

"What was it?"

"I put a Christmas candle in it one year. My mom found it under my pillow and had a fit though."

"Is that all?"

"Well, I've got a Super-Size Sharpie I stick in there sometimes when I jack off."

Jason grinned.

"Kinky," he said.

"Well just think of my perfect cock as a flesh colored sharpie."

Jason squirted some lube on his cock and then put some on Paul's butt hole. He took his finger and rubbed it and then slid his finger in. Paul gasped.

"Are you okay?"

"Yeah, it feels so good," he said.

"Better than a Sharpie?"

"Oh way better."

"Oh if you like that, you'll love this," Jason said wagging his cock.

He moved forward and put his cock at Paul's hole. Manny was sitting on the bed next to Trevor and me and his cock was hard again. He reached over absentmindedly and started playing with my cock.

"Okay, here we go," Jason said.

He pushed and Paul groaned. Jason let up and then he pushed again. Paul groaned but Jason's dick head slid in. Paul jumped and gasped but didn't ask for it to be taken out. He closed his eyes tightly.

"Are you okay?" Jason asked.

"It hurts pretty bad."

"Just let it like this for a bit. See if it stops hurting."

They held like that for a bit. Manny was mesmerized watching them. He lay over and began sucking my cock while he watched. Trevor looked down and grinned.

"I was planning on that," he said quietly.

"Stand up," I said.

Trevor grinned and stood up so his boner was at my face. I took it into my mouth just as Paul nodded to Jason.

"Put more in," he said.

Jason worked in a little more cock and slowly but surely he got the whole damn thing in there. Paul had his eyes closed and looked like he loved it.

"Are you okay Paul?" Trevor asked.

"Oh man, that's way better than a Super-Sized Sharpie."

We all began laughing and Manny nearly choked on my cock. Jason began fucking Paul slowly. It was pretty damn erotic seeing this little guy who looked so young and innocent with a big cock stuck up his ass. His cock was standing up hard as a rock and precum was running from it like a faucet.

"Manny, give Paul a little head," I said.

Manny took my cock from his mouth and went to work on Paul's. Trevor lay down on the bed next to me facing the other way and we sucked each other. Jason increased his speed and I knew it was time.

"Manny, get him off," I said.

Manny took Paul deeply and I saw the little guy's eyes flutter and thought he might have passed out. Manny gulped and I knew Paul was having the orgasm of his life. He began to make sounds like a cat meowing.

Jason pushed in as far as he could get and held and I knew he was cumming.

I stuck my finger in Trevor's ass and he yelped and his cock shot cum into my mouth. Manny was jacking himself while he slurped on Paul's cock and he shot cum all over the floor. I was the only one who hadn't cum.

Trevor was sucking me fast and Manny pinched my tits. Jason pulled his cock out of Paul and began to kiss me and sucked on my tongue and I let a blast go into Trevor's mouth. He sucked me dry and we all lay back on the beds panting.

I looked over at little Paul and he was smiling and sweating like mad.

"Are you okay little man?"

"Oh man. That was the best cum of my life. Oh fuck. I'll never forget that as long as I live."

"I think he liked it," Jason said.

"*Bueno*," Manny added.

"Let's go shower," Trevor suggested.

We all got up. Our cocks were wet and red and hanging in every state from nearly fully boned to limp. We all grabbed towels and walked to the shower.

"Thanks for that," Paul said.

"More to come," Jason said. He put his arm around the little guy and kissed him on the cheek.

"Glad you enjoyed it," Manny said. "Maybe next time you can try a grown-up cock."

Jason grabbed him and they were wrestling on the floor of the shower with water cascading over them. Damn wrestlers.

THE NEXT day, the coach announced that we'd scrimmage instead of run the stairs. There were no complaints about that. We gathered in the gym and sat on the edge of the wrestling mat and the coach paired us up to see what moves we had.

Manny and Jason were first and they were pretty equally matched. Chris and Dave also got paired up. Dave got Chris on his back with a cool move and pretty much got the best of him.

Two heavy weights were next. It was like watching a couple of those big elephant seals rolling around. As big as they were they were pretty agile and they had a good match.

Trevor was next and he got paired up with a kid we didn't know real well. He had no trouble with him and pinned him in no time.

Then it was my turn. I got paired with a kid who weighed the same as me but was about 8 inches taller. He had long arms and legs and I found out pretty quickly he had a lot of leverage. I made a stupid move and he got me on my back. He had me in a half nelson and had one arm around my neck when he put his other hand in my crotch.

It is a normal move to crotch-hold in wrestling. Normally you get your hand in deep into the crotch of your opponent and hold him by his upper thigh. This kid had his hand right on my cock and balls and was squeezing them.

"Fuck," I said.

"Sorry."

I worked hard to keep from getting pinned and he held onto my cock all the while. Finally I made a move and reversed him. He was on his back and I was on top of him. I put in a crotch hold and damn... he had a boner! I looked at him and he looked embarrassed.

He let off and I pinned him. We shook hands and he hurried off the mat and went for the locker room.

When I sat down Trevor leaned over.

"Did he have hard-on?"

I nodded.

"I could see it," he said.

Manny was sitting across from us and he was grinning. He took his hand and made a jacking motion. I grinned at him and he got up and trotted off to the locker room.

"Manny is on the prowl."

Chapter Six

After everyone had wrestled the coach let us go for the day. There was no afternoon practice and the next day was Sunday so there was no practice then either. We were told the gym would be open for workouts on our own and so would the pool and sauna.

When we went in to shower I saw the kid I'd wrestled and he was talking to Manny. I saw Manny look toward me and then at Trevor and he said something to the kid. They nodded and Manny came jogging over.

"We have a new player," he said.

"What?"

"That kid you wrestled? The one you molested? He likes to play."

"Molested! I didn't molest him you little brown Shitbird. If anyone molested anyone, he molested me."

Manny laughed and stripped off his tee shirt.

"Oh, don't get your panties in a bunch. He'd like to play with us."

"Well sure," I said.

"Why don't we all go to the lake?" Trevor said.

"Cool idea," Manny said.

He pulled off his shorts and walked naked back to the kid. He told him our plans and then walked over to Chris and Dave and Cody and soon they all were grinning and heading for the shower. Jason was wondering what was going on and Trevor told him. He had a big smile on his face and was semi-boned up as he walked to the shower.

"Damn this is going to be epic," he said as he walked past.

We were just about to leave the locker room when Paul came hustling in.

"Coach kept me after to show me a move," he said out of breath.

"We're going to the lake," I said.

"Oh, okay," he said.

"Come with us."

"Can I really?"

"Of course," I said.

"You four?"

"Chris and Dave and that tall kid and Cody are going too."

"Cody's into it too?"

"Yup."

"Damn are there any straight guys on the wrestling team?"

I grinned.

"Not many it seems."

"I wonder if I could get some of that Cialis stuff? Jason said as we drove to the lake. We were in two cars and he and Trevor, Manny, Paul and me were in my car and the others including the new kid, Kerry were in Dave's car.

"What that stuff to make you get a boner?" Trevor asked.

"Yeah, I'd like to get some of that."

"What the hell do you need that for? You've got a boner most of the day as it is," I said.

"Have you ever seen that commercial? They say something about a boner lasting four hours. Now that's something I'd like, an eternal boner.

"You idiot, as horny as you are, you'd probably never get soft. That's a bad thing to have a four-hour boner."

"Bad why? Just think of the fucking I could do."

Manny shook his head.

"Does insanity run in your family?"

Jason grinned.

"No but you can blow me if you like on the way."

Manny laughed and then reached into Jason's pants and hauled out his cock and leaned over and started blowing him.

"Jeez, what the hell?" I said. "What if someone sees and calls a cop?"

"Oh don't get your wiener in a sling. If you get pulled over we'll plead insanity."

Trevor just grinned.

"So sad to see juvenile mental disease," he said.

WE GOT to the beach and there were a few people there, so we decided to play football in the water. Since there were nine of us we chose up sides and ended up with Chris, Trevor, Kerry and me on one team and Manny, Cody, Dave, Paul and Jason on the other.

We had a hell of a lot of fun but it was really tiring running in the water. It just happened often that someone's swimming trunks ended up getting pulled off too. It was getting late in the day and the last of the other swimmers left.

"So?" Manny said.

"So what?"

"How about naked football?"

"What if someone comes?" Dave asked.

"I expect that," Manny said.

"No I mean comes, like in arrives," Dave said.

"Oh, well we'll just sit down in the water and they won't know."

Well that made a lot of sense.

We all ran out on the sand and stripped off our swimming trunks. Kerry was boned up already. He had a pretty nice cock on him too.

We started playing and it was soon obvious that the game had changed. Now when someone got tackled or blocked there was a lot of grabbing of cocks and balls and a lot of fingers inserted into butt cracks.

Soon we all had boners and were laughing like mad every play. My team had the ball and I passed it to Chris. He took off running and Jason tackled him. They went under water and when Chris came up Jason had his arms wrapped around his waist and had his cock in his mouth.

"He's like a fucking Piranha," Chris said laughing.

Jason looked up and grinned and then he went back to Chris' cock. The rest of us stood there and finally Manny waded over to Kerry, the new kid and said something. They walked out of the water and Kerry lay on the sand and Manny knelt between his legs and began sucking him.

It must have been quite a sight. There were nine boys, some sucking one while the other watched and some doing a sixty-nine on the beach. I was with Dave, Trevor was with Cody and the others were already paired up. It was pretty hot. It took fifteen minutes and it seemed that everyone had cum. We all lay back resting and grinning.

"Damn will you look at this?" Manny said.

"I never thought there were this many gay guys anywhere especially in a group like our wrestling team."

"We're bi," Dave said.

"Okay, still nine cock suckers?"

"Maybe there are more than people think," Trevor said.

"You know," Dave said, "there are some guys who like to show off. They wear tank tops to show off their muscles and they wear tight jeans to show off their junk. I think wrestlers are a lot like that."

"They like showing off their bodies," Trevor said nodding.

"Yeah, look at what we wear to wrestle in," Kerry said.

We all nodded and grinned.

"It's like being naked on the mat. All we wear is a pair of boxer briefs and a tank top but it's in one piece."

"You're right. There's no imagination needed to figure out what a guy's cock looks like in that get-up."

"So guys, who like others to see their cock, gravitate to wrestling."

"It makes sense," I said.

"What do you think Jason?" I asked.

"I've got sand in my ass crack," Jason said.

We all laughed.

"Hey I've got an idea, how about back to the gym and then a shower and a sauna?" Manny suggested.

Everyone liked that idea.

"Let's stop for pizza on the way," Kerry said. "I'm starved."

"I'll call the Pizza Depot, and have some ready and we can pick them up," Trevor said.

So we wiped as much sand off us as we could and then put on our swimming trunks and piled into the cars. We pooled our money and stopped and picked up four large pizzas and four two-liter bottles of soda and headed to the gym.

The doors were left unlocked so we went in.The place was empty. So we hurried into the showers and all rinsed off the sand and then we went out to the pool area and sat naked eating pizza. We all laughed and talked like it was an everyday thing for nine naked guys to have a pizza party. I was getting to like this college thing.

After the pizza was gone we drifted into the sauna. We were pretty full from eating and sat and lay on the benches and enjoyed the warmth. Cody poured some water on the stones and made a bunch of steam. Everyone began to sweat.

I looked around me. Damn there were eight cute guys, all of them naked, all glistening with sweat and it was pretty erotic. I began boning up.

"Need a hand with that?"

I turned and it was Trevor. He smiled his beautiful smile and I leaned forward and kissed him.

"Yeah," I said quietly.

Trevor took hold of my cock and jacked me slowly. I put my arms around him and hugged him to me.

Everyone was getting into it on the benches. There were a couple of guys sucking and Manny was licking Kerry's asshole. Jason had his legs up in the air and Cody was lubing up a condom. Damn.

"Let's go someplace more private," Trevor said.

We got up and walked to the locker room. Trevor led me to the shower and we turned on a couple of spigots.

He put his arms around me and we began kissing. Our boners were rubbing together and it was very sexy.

"There's one thing you haven't done yet," he said.

I nodded.

"With all the new guys it kind of got lost in the shuffle."

"I want to do it now," he said.

"There's no one I'd rather do it with than you, Trev."

We kissed and hugged hard.

Trevor had a condom in his hand that he'd brought from the sauna. He ripped it open and rolled it down my cock.

"We'll have to use spit," he said.

"No problem."

"How do you want me?" he asked.

"I want us to face each other," I said.

He smiled and lay on the floor of the shower with water cascading over him. He lifted up his legs and I looked down at his beautiful cock, balls and hole. Damn he was gorgeous.

I knelt down and sucked his cock and then licked his balls. He closed his eyes and let out a moan. Then I lapped at his sweet hole.

"Oh Micah, make love to me," he said.

I moved up and put my cock up to his hole. He closed his eyes as I pushed the head in. I stopped when it went in so he could get used to it.

"I'm okay," he said looking up.

I put my cock in him slowly and in a minute it was all the way to my pubes. He wrapped his legs around me and I began fucking him slowly. I leaned down and we kissed. He sucked on my tongue and pinched my tits.

"Oh your cock is so thick, it feels amazing," he whispered.

"Trev, I think I'm falling for you," I said.

He looked up at me and smiled.

"I know I'm falling for you Micah."

We made love quietly and gently. After many minutes I felt my cock get the feeling and I went in deep and let it cum. Trevor squeezed me with his legs and I emptied my cum into the condom in his ass.

I collapsed on top of him and we lay there kissing.

"That was beautiful," he said.

"Not as beautiful as you are," I said.

"Well will you look at this?"

We looked up and there were Manny and Jason looking down at us. Manny was stroking Jason's cock.

"What?" I said.

"Private party?"

"Making love," I said.

They grinned.

"We've been watching you two. We knew that was happening," Jason said.

"Is it okay with you two?" Trevor asked.

"Damn straight, as long as we get to suck those cocks now and then."

"Come and join us," Trevor said patting the floor next to him.

The two little shits scurried over and lay down and began playing with Trevor's cock and balls. Manny pulled the condom off me and licked the cum off my cock. Then he began to suck me and I got hard again.

"Damn Mexican cock suckers," I said.

Manny grinned.

"Si Senior."

Sunday morning we all slept in late. We were pretty tired after all the practice, swimming and fucking the day before. We missed breakfast so we made sure to get to the food center for lunch.

The four of us were sitting at a table eating when Chris and Dave came in. They stopped at our table.

"So what's up for the day?" I asked.

"Our girlfriends are coming to visit. We have to service them I suppose."

"Ugh, pussy," Manny said.

"Well, some of us like it too,' Chris said.

"Have fun."

Paul came in a bit later alone and spotted us. We waved him over.

"How's it hanging Paulie?" Jason asked.

"It's kind of sore."

We laughed.

"Overwork it yesterday?"

He nodded.

"But if anything is going on today I'm in," he said.

Horny little shit.

"What are we gonna do?" Manny asked.

Jason got an evil smirk on his face.

"How about naked Twister?"

"Naked Twister?"

He nodded.

"Ever play Twister? Same thing except everyone is naked. It's fun."

"Paulie, what do you think?"

He reached down and adjusted his cock in his pants.

"I like it," he said.

Chapter Seven

We couldn't find the rest of the gang so we went back to our room. Jason had a Twister mat in his dresser and he got it out. We laid it on the floor and he got out the spinner.

"Ok, everybody! Get naked," he said.

We all stripped down. Paul had a boner on already.

"Are you excited?" Manny asked.

He nodded.

"I've been saving up for something like this for 18 years."

Manny went first. He got a right foot blue. He stepped out onto the mat with his right foot on a blue dot.

Next was Trevor. He got a left hand red.

Then it was my turn. I got right foot yellow

And on we went. Soon it got interesting. Once we had more than one appendage on the mat it got more difficult to move with others in the way.

About the third move Paul got left hand green. He was spread out with one foot on one side of the mat and the other on the opposite side. He had to put his hand on green and the only open green was behind Jason.

Paul leaned under Jason and put his hand on the spot but Jason's cock and balls were resting on his back. Jason grinned and closed his eyes.

Suddenly, Jason let a fart right on Paul's back. Paul jerked up and he and Jason fell off the mat laughing. Paul grabbed Jason in a wrestling move and soon they were all wrapped up legs and arms everywhere. We knew where this was going.

Paul got behind Jason and his boner was right in Jason's ass crack.

"I'll give you fifteen minutes to stop that," Jason said.

"Okay," Paul said and got off him.

"No, I was kidding. I liked it back there," Jason said.

"I've never," Paul said.

"Oh shit, you've never fucked before have you?" Manny said. He was sitting on the mat between Trevor's legs with his face right in Trev's crotch.

"No, not yet." Paul said.

"No time like the present," Jason said. "It you want to."

Paul looked at us watching him.

"Here?"

"We won' tell," Manny said.

Paul grinned.

"Okay with you Jason?"

"Fuck yeah."

Jason picked the smallest condom since Paul's cock wasn't real huge. He rolled it down and lubed him up. Then he lubed his asshole.

"How do you want to do it?" he asked.

"I think from behind," Paul said.

'Okey dokey," Jason said and got on his hands and knees.

Paul moved in behind him with his five-inch boner in his hand. He looked at the three of us, now sitting on the opposite bed watching.

"So I just put it in?"

"Go slow so he can get used to it," Trevor said.

I looked at Trevor and smiled. He was making the little guy feel good thinking his little cock would hurt Jason. The truth was that Jason had Manny's big thick Mexican cock in his ass so many times he could take Paul's with no trouble. But it was good to give him confidence and not make him feel like he was inadequate.

He put the head at Jason's hole and it went right in. Jason moaned and we knew it was acting but Paul didn't.

Soon Paul was balls-to-the-wall and fucking like a little jackrabbit. His little balls were swinging back and forth and he had a look on his face like he was in heaven.

"Oh Paul, that's amazing," Jason said.

"Are you okay?"

"I'm good, I love it."

We smiled and Trevor and I had a kiss. Manny was stroking his big brown cock. He looked over at us and smiled.

"You two are good together."

We nodded.

"Why don't you get Jason off?" I said.

Manny grinned and got up and slid under Jason and took his cock in his mouth. Jason's balls were swinging back and forth and hit Manny in the forehead.

"I'm about to cum," Paul panted.

"Let it go,' Jason said.

Trevor and I were stroking each other and kissing. It was hard not to get excited watching what was going on the other bed.

Paul pushed into Jason and held it and made a whimpering sound. He was cumming.

Manny took Jason deep into his mouth and Jason grunted. Manny began swallowing so we knew he was cumming too.

Manny got out from under Jason and he collapsed on the bed with Paul still inside him. Manny stood there with his big boner throbbing. Paul looked up and grabbed it and started sucking it.

Trevor and I were pretty hot now and I felt my cock getting close.

"I'm about there, Trev," I said.

He leaned down and took it in his mouth and went deep on me and I came. He sucked it dry and licked my balls and then sat up. We kissed.

"Lay back," I said.

Trevor lay back against the bed and I went on his cock with my mouth. I love his cock. I took it deeply into my throat and milked it with my throat muscles. He moaned when I did that and a few seconds later he came. I sucked every drop from it. Then I licked his cock off and licked his big balls.

Manny began talking Spanish. Paul had half of his big cock in his mouth and suddenly he jerked. Cum squirted out of the side of his mouth as Manny came. Paul was a trooper though and didn't get off that cock. He slurped up the rest and then licked of the overflow from Manny's balls and his cheek.

We all were sweating and breathing hard and Jason said, "Well that kind of shoots the naked Twister game in the ass."

The five of us went to dinner and ate and had a good time. If nothing else we'd all become good friends in the previous week and we had something to look forward to in the upcoming months of school.

When we finished Paul decided to go to his room and rest. The little guy seemed like he was walking on air. I think his first fuck changed him a bit.

The other four of us got to the dorm and Jason stopped.

"Manny and I were thinking maybe we could switch roommates for the night."

I looked at Trevor and he smiled.

"Sure, that'd be good," I said.

Manny and Jason grinned as they walked toward my room. The little shits were as horny as any I'd ever seen but I think they cooked up this switch so Trevor and I could be together.

"Did they fool you?" Trevor asked as we walked into his room.

"You mean Manny and Jason? They wanted us together I think."

He nodded.

"Manny has been pestering me about being in love with you," he said blushing.

"He said that to me too."

"And?"

I put my arms around this most beautiful boy. We kissed and lay on the bed in each other's arms.

"I think he's right Trevor. I think I've fallen in love with you."

"Manny is very perceptive for a little shit head."

I laughed.

"Those two are so cute together. They're lucky to have found each other."

"I'm lucky to have found you too Micah. I never thought I'd actually love another boy. I hoped to find someone to have sex with on a regular basis but never thought I'd really fall in love."

"And you have?"

He kissed me deeply and I could feel his hard cock grinding into mine.

"Yes I have."

We took our time. Over the next hour or so we got naked, kissed, sucked and made love. Then we lay in each other's arms naked.

"Well, tomorrow the upperclassmen come to camp," I said.

"I wonder how many of them are gay?"

"Damn I wonder too. If there are as many as there are in the freshman class we'll have a damn cock loving team."

"I don't need any other cock from now on," he said kissing me.

"Me either."

Trevor fell asleep first. I looked at him. He was as handsome as any boy I knew… and he loved me. Damn, how lucky could a guy get?

The End

Here is a sample from another story you may enjoy:

Dick Parker

CANADIAN
HOOK-UP
Gay Erotica

If I'd had my choice of fishing partners, I'd have probably chosen someone a little closer to my own age. I was in a van with my grandpa and two of his cronies on my way to a fly-in fishing trip in Canada.

My dad died when I was a young teenager and my Grandpa Fred had taken over the job of being both a grandpa and a dad. He saw to it that I learned about life and the outdoors and was the most important man in my life.

Grandpa Fred and three of his buddies had been taking a fishing trip to Canada every spring for decades. They went the first time when they were just out of college and had been going ever since. Last winter one of the old guys died in his sleep so there was an opening in the fishing quartet. Grandpa asked me to go along and take his place.

I was flattered that the three of them wanted me to go along. I liked them all. They were funny old guys who knew how to have a good time. They'd been friends since their college days and were real characters. The only problem was that they were all in their early seventies. I had just turned 20.

The other problem was that I was gay. No one knew of my sexual preference and I hoped to keep it that way. I'd made it through high school and two years of college telling the people around me that I spent all of my time studying so I'd get good grades. I said that I just didn't have time for a woman right now. So far, I'd gotten away with it.

The truth was that I didn't want a woman. I wanted a boyfriend. Oh I'd had some jack off sessions with a few buddies but I'd never done anything more than that. I remember one time two buddies and I were watching a porn video and someone had suggested we all jack off. I didn't have a boner when we were watching because it was straight porn but as soon as one of the guys got his hard cock out I had a boner like right now. That was the highlight of my sexual experience in my first twenty years. I probably jacked off to that memory a hundred times. I never had the guts to try something with a boy because I was terrified that someone would find out and I'd be labeled a queer, or a sissy boy. It would have hurt my grandpa's feelings to know he had a gay grandson and I loved the old man too much to take the chance of it happening. So, here I was on my way to Canada with a gang of old-farts instead of on my way to Florida with a gang of cunt hunters.

"So Caleb, what's the woman situation at your school?" my grandpa's friend Herb asked.

"Oh there are lots of pretty ones," I said. "Most of the really cute ones are taken or bitches."

"I hear you," Herb said laughing. "They always say marry an ugly woman, she'll be lots easier to get along with and grateful as hell." The three old farts laughed their butts off and so did I.

"I'll ask your wife if that's the way it is when we get back," I said.

"Oh damn, no. Don't you dare tell her that I said something like that. She'll have my balls hanging around her neck."

"She'll cut you off," Grandpa's other friend Lenny said.

"She cut me off twenty years ago," Herb said. "Even when I get my semi-annual boner she's usually too tired." We all laughed crazily when he said that.

"I don't worry though." He held up his hand and made a jacking motion.

"I can get my friend Rosie Palm and her five sisters to help me out any time I like."

They roared with laughter. My face turned red. Damn these guys were in their seventies and they were talking about jacking off? I thought only teenagers and young guys did that kind of stuff.

"What? You look surprised," Lenny said.

"I just didn't think...I guess that just surprised me," I stammered.

"You think once you get old you don't get boners?" Herb asked.

"Well, I suppose... jeez can we talk about something else?"

They laughed and laughed and I had to grin. What a bunch of characters.

"Caleb, you know they did a study a while back. They interviewed ten thousand men and boys. They asked them if they jacked off or not. You know what they found out?"

Oh boy I hated to ask but I said, "No, what?"

"They found out that 92 percent of men and boys jack off. They also found that eight percent of men and boys are LIARS!" They laughed about that one for miles.

We drove on through the night. Once it got dark I volunteered to drive. Their eyesight wasn't what it once was and I felt safer if it was me driving instead of one of these old guys.

We stopped at a roadside diner about seven in the morning and got out. Everyone stretched and groaned after being on the road all night. Herb let a loud fart and the three of them had a big laugh over that.

We went into the diner and sat in a booth. A girl who looked about my age came to take our order. She was writing the orders on a pad and Lenny elbowed me. He wiggled his eyebrows and motioned toward the girl's tits.

I grinned at him and nodded that I'd noticed them. The girl left and Lenny whispered to me, "I bet there's a couple of puppies with brown noses in there."

I didn't know for sure what to say.

"She's too young for you," I said.

"No, she's perfect for you."

"Lenny, what am I supposed to do? Walk into the kitchen and haul out my dick and screw her?"

"I bet that'd make her day," he said.

The three of them howled with laughter.

I heard the bell on the door ring and two young guys came in and took a booth across from us. They were young, maybe 18 or 19 and looked like they'd been out all night. They were both nice looking kids with longer hair and were dressed like they'd just come from a party.

I noticed them because they were cute as hell. I kept watching them out of the corner of my eye. The waitress took their order and left. Then one of them reached across and took the other's hand in his. They smiled and the other one made an air kiss to the first one.

Damn. They must be boyfriends.

One got up and went to the bathroom. Our food came and we began eating. I saw the kid coming back and when he got to the booth he bent down and the two kids kissed quickly.

He sat down and the one who'd been sitting looked and saw me watching. I smiled and he gave me a grin. He said something to the other and he turned and winked at me.

"Did you see that?" Lenny asked.

"What's that?" Grandpa asked.

"That kid over there. He kissed the other one."

Grandpa and Herb turned and looked.

"Is that one on our side with her back to us a girl?"

"Nope. She's a boy, too."

They turned and looked again.

"Hmmm. Well, it is what it is," Grandpa said.

WE WERE finishing up and I had to pee so I went to the bathroom while the others paid the bill and got in the van. I was holding my dick peeing when the door opened and the other kid from the booth walked up to the next urinal.

"What's up?" he said, hauling his dick out.

"Not much, how's it going with you?"

He pulled on his dick a couple of times and began peeing. He made no pretense of looking at my dick while he pissed.

"My friend and I are on our way home from a long night," he said. "We partied long and hard."

"I noticed you guys when you came in," I said. "Are you a couple?"

He grinned. 'You saw the kiss?"

I nodded.

"Tony is pretty brave. We've just started um, having sex and he thinks everyone will be okay with it."

"I'm fine with it," I said. He looked at my dick and then at his. I followed his eyes to his and it was half hard. He grinned at me.

"I like your cock," he said. "It's pretty thick."

"Yeah, it bones up pretty fat," I said. "You guys up here don't get cut much, do you?" He pulled his foreskin back and showed me his cock, which was now nearly fully hard.

"We like to keep natural," he said as he stroked it a little.

My cock began to bone up. He grinned.

"Getting a little excited," he said.

"Damn, I wish I had a little more time," I said. "My friends are waiting for me."

"Too bad, Tony noticed you too. We thought we might have a party." Damn. I shoved my cock back in my pants.

"You can't imagine how much I'd like that but I have to go," I said. He shrugged. I turned and reached over and put my hand on his big hard cock and pulled on it.

"Damn," I said.

"What the hell took so long?" Herb asked.

"I had to piss," I said.

"That had to be the longest piss of the year," Lenny added.

"Let's go," Grandpa said.

WE ARRIVED at the border a little before noon. We went through customs and just a little way down the road on the Canadian side there was an information place so we stopped to get a map.

There was a really beautiful girl in the place and she was the official welcome from Canada. She was a blond with short gorgeous hair, blue eyes and a great figure, and she was wearing white shorts, a white blouse and a red blazer. She was a beauty, even for a gay guy like me. The old-farts nearly had a coronary when they saw her.

She gave us all kinds of information and I thought Herb was going to drool on the counter. We thanked her and went back to the van.

"Holy Hannah," Herb said. "My old wiener liked that."

I felt my face getting red.

"Caleb, pull off somewhere and let me out. I gotta go and let off some sexual tension." I looked over my shoulder and didn't know if he was kidding or not.

"Keep it in your pants, Lenny," Grandpa said. "We haven't got all day to wait for you to get it up again. We have to be at the pick-up place in an hour."

"I don't need to get it up again. It's up!"

"Well, keep it in your pants. I sure as hell don't want to see that shriveled up old dick of yours and I don't think anyone else does either," Grandpa said.

"I might like to watch," Lenny said. We all laughed like mad. Damn what a bunch of oversexed old-farts.

THE LODGE we were going to was on a lake nearly a hundred miles in the bush. All fishermen and all of the food and other stuff had to be flown in on floatplanes. We had to meet one of them at a dock and load our stuff onto it and then ride into the lake with the pilot.

I'd never flown before so it was pretty exciting for me. We arrived and there were six other cars and vans parked in the lot. We unloaded our fishing rods and clothes and piled it on the dock.

"Well here we are," Grandpa said.

"Are you excited, Caleb?"

"Yeah, Grandpa," I said, "thanks for bringing me." The old man put his arm around my shoulder.

"I wish your dad could be here. He'd be really proud of the fine young man you've grown up to be."

I saw some tears in his eyes. He was devastated when my dad died. He'd been there for me all my life and now he was getting old and I hated the idea of losing him someday.

"Here they come," Lenny said pointing to the north.

We all looked and I saw an orange thing in the sky that kept getting closer and closer. The plane circled the lake and came in from the east. There was a west wind so I supposed he liked to land into the wind.

He landed and taxied across the lake to the dock. When he got up close he turned the tail and the plane turned parallel to the dock. The engine shut down and the door opened and a kid jumped out and grabbed a rope that was tied to the front pontoon and tied it to a cleat on the dock. Then he sprinted back and did the same on the back. He turned around and smiled at us.

"You must be my fishermen?"

"Does your daddy know you took his plane, sonny?" Lenny asked.

"My boss does, sir. I'm the pilot. I guarantee I know how to fly."

I must have looked shocked. He was beautiful. I stood there with my mouth hanging open. The others began picking up gear and I stood there looking at the kid.

If you enjoyed this sample then look for **Canadian Hook-up.**

Also by this Author:

About the Author

Dick Parker is an outdoorsman and has lived in the mid-west all of his life. His favorite activities are fishing, hunting and sex with other guys. He found out at a young age that he was gay and has had many outdoor adventures with friends that turned into more than just a fishing trip.

He began writing outdoor stories for sporting magazines and then delved into erotic stories. A lot of the situations in the stories are from personal experiences. He writes full time and is always willing to do research for a new story idea.

From the Author

Check my page on Amazon for Updates and interesting info.

Author Central - http://www.amazon.com/Dick-Parker/e/B00CHWL2AG

If you enjoyed any of my books then please share the love and click like on my books in Amazon.

If you write me a review and send me an email I will send you a free book, or many.
(Just know that these emails are filtered by my publisher.)

Good news is always welcome.

One Last Thing, For Kindle Readers...

When you turn the page, Kindle will give you the opportunity to rate this book and share your thoughts on Facebook and Twitter. If you enjoyed my writings, would you please take a few seconds to let your friends know about it? Because... when they enjoy they will be grateful to you and so will I.

Thank You!

Dick Parker
dick_parker@awesomeauthors.org